Samuel French Acting

All the Fine Boys

by Erica Schmidt

SAMUELFRENCH.COM   SAMUELFRENCH.CO.UK

MUSIC USE NOTE

Licensees are solely responsible for obtaining formal written permission from copyright owners to use copyrighted music in the performance of this play and are strongly cautioned to do so. If no such permission is obtained by the licensee, then the licensee must use only original music that the licensee owns and controls. Licensees are solely responsible and liable for all music clearances and shall indemnify the copyright owners of the play(s) and their licensing agent, Samuel French, against any costs, expenses, losses and liabilities arising from the use of music by licensees. Please contact the appropriate music licensing authority in your territory for the rights to any incidental music.

IMPORTANT BILLING AND CREDIT REQUIREMENTS

If you have obtained performance rights to this title, please refer to your licensing agreement for important billing and credit requirements.

ALL THE FINE BOYS was first produced by The New Group at The Ford Studio Theater at The Signature in New York City from February 14 to March 26, 2017. The production was directed by Erica Schmidt, with scenic design by Amy Rubin, costume design by Tom Broecker, lighting design by Jeff Croiter, and sound design by Bart Fasbender. The Production Stage Manager was Jillian Oliver. The cast was as follows:

JOSEPH..Joe Tippett

JENNY... Abigail Breslin

ADAM .... Alex Wolff

EMILY ....Isabelle Fuhrman

CHARACTERS

JOSEPH – Twenty-eight, blonde, blue eyes, very handsome in a traditional kind of way: button-down shirt, khaki pants, loafers, well-combed hair, favors sunglasses, seems very adult, likes motorcycles, football, and skeet shooting, works at the local power plant. A religious, middle-class, suburban, southern man.

JENNY – Fourteen, skinny, sometimes sunny, sometimes stormy.

ADAM – Seventeen, the cool kid, the first alternative, dark hair, tall, thin, very smart, well-read, the lead in the high school play, and the editor of the literary magazine. A musician; an actor and a poet. Really.

EMILY – Fourteen, a sponge, listens to everything, a little bit heavy (she already has boobs), a little bit pretty.

SETTING

Suburban South Carolina

TIME

Late 1980s

AUTHOR'S NOTES

The passages of time indicated as "Beat'" are transitions. For performance, these transitions should occur very quickly – like a pulse or a breath. An en dash (–) indicates a cutting off or speeding up of thought. An elipsis (...) indicates a trailing off or slowing down. The dialogue in parentheses is meant to be spoken aloud (in a parenthetical way).

A second note: anything you think is a joke, probably is.

TIMELINE
(for folks who like timelines...)

APRIL 29 – Friday night. Jenny and Emily sleepover.

MAY 14 – Saturday night. Jenny's dad's church party, where Emily spends the night and Jenny sees Joseph.

MAY 24 – Tuesday after school. Jenny and Joseph: Scenes 1 and 1.5, and Adam and Emily: Scene A.

MAY 25 – Wednesday morning and evening. Jenny and Joseph: Scene 2, Jenny calls Emily. Adam and Emily: Scene B, "But she cut school today."

MAY 26 – Thursday.

MAY 27 – Friday. Jenny and Joseph: Scene 3, "My birthday is tomorrow." She calls her mom and the play opens for Emily and Adam.

MAY 28 – Saturday. Jenny and Joseph: Scene 4, Jenny's birthday.

MAY 29 – Sunday. Closing night party for the play.

MAY 30 – Monday. Adam and Emily: Scene C, "She's missed four days of school," "She missed the play," "She missed her birthday."

JUNE 4 – Adam and Emily: Scene D, Adam's birthday.

JUNE 19 – Graduation.

JULY – A year later. Adam and Emily: Scene E.

The passage of time could be indicated by Joseph, Emily, and Adam changing clothes.

Emily and Jenny

(The basement of a suburban home. Late April in the late 1980s. In the middle of the unfinished room a pull-out couch has been made into a bed-fort stacked with mismatched pillows, blankets, and sleeping bags. An old 1970s-style television set and video player sit on a table facing the bed. A big shag carpet sticks out from under the couch/bed. A staircase leads up into the kitchen and the rest of the house beyond.
EMILY *[fourteen] is sitting on the bed reading* The Bell Jar; **JENNY** *[fourteen] comes down the stairs carrying a very tall stack of videos and sets them on the VCR.)*

JENNY. Why is there nothing to eat in my god damn house?

EMILY. We could go to the store?

JENNY. On our bikes?

EMILY. Why not?

JENNY. Lame.

EMILY. Nah-uh.

JENNY. It's Friday night. What if some high school kids see us?

EMILY. I don't care. I like my bike.

JENNY. Nerd.

EMILY. *(Shy.)* I might have brought provisions.

JENNY. What?–What–What–What??

> *(**EMILY** rummages in her backpack and produces a red can of Pringles.)*

EMILY. Ta-da!

JENNY. Yes!!

EMILY. What did your mom rent us?

JENNY. *(Going to the pile of movies and reading:) A Stranger is Watching, Bloody Birthday, Chopping Mall, Bloody Cheerleader Camp, Dead Ringers, Children of the Corn, Eyes of a Stranger,* and *I Spit on Your Grave.*

EMILY. Wow.

JENNY. Yup.

EMILY. What do you want to watch first?

JENNY. Toss-up. Either *Bloody Birthday* or *I Spit on Your Grave.*

EMILY. I think I saw *Bloody Birthday.*

JENNY. When?

EMILY. Kristen's birthday-sleep-over-thing. (Sorry.)

JENNY. What? – Don't be sorry – I told you – I don't care. Why'd you even go to that?

EMILY. I like her.

JENNY. She doesn't like you.

EMILY. Yes she does.

JENNY. She doesn't act like it at school.

EMILY. She's just popular.

JENNY. She only hangs around the dancer girls.

EMILY. She's in the Southern Strut – those are her friends.

JENNY. But we're not in Strut.

EMILY. I think next year, I'm *not* going to try out.

JENNY. I stopped trying out when I was like eight.

EMILY. I think maybe I'm not meant to be a dancer.

JENNY. It's true. Not everyone can dance on *Star Search.*

EMILY. They really are sooooo good.

JENNY. *(With a sigh.)* Yeah.

EMILY. I still think she's cool, Kristen.

JENNY. Do you think your house will get toilet-papered again tonight?

EMILY. I hope not. My dad was so mad last weekend. He's started making me clean it up – by myself. He woke me up at like, six – awful.

JENNY. You never get all that toilet paper down. Your house looks, like, haunted.

EMILY. I know.

JENNY. I heard it was John Pains' brother that did it last weekend.

EMILY. But I'm friends with Brian.

JENNY. So? That's why they do it at night so no one knows how secretly they hate you.

EMILY. That's not it at all. The whole thing is 'cause I just moved here and 'cause I have boobs.

(**JENNY** *laughs.*)

It's true! When they prank call they always say, 'slut' – like in a whisper and – oh my god! – I didn't tell you – two weekends ago they wrote 'slut' in shaving cream on the driveway – my dad got the hose out – he was so mad. Just staring at me and spraying the driveway and shaking his head. I don't know why he gets mad at me though? I don't even want my boobs. I hate when he doesn't say anything. My dad? I come into a room. He leaves.

JENNY. He just doesn't know what to make of you, like – who you are – I bet he's freaked by your boobs too.

EMILY. Shut up!

JENNY. No really. They're huge.

EMILY. I hate my boobs. It's true! My mom makes me buy clothes in, like, the maternity section –

(*They both laugh.*)

JENNY. Well, no matter how big those boobs are, they have an end.

EMILY. That's comforting. My body is finite. I looked it up in the dictionary, you know? (Slut): 'dirty or slovenly, a woman who is considered to have loose sexual morals or who is sexually promiscuous. The term is pejorative and used as an insult, sexual slur or offensive disparagement.' I mean –

JENNY. That's why your dad is mad. He probably thinks you actually *are* a slut.

EMILY. I think that now – mostly – my house is just the house everyone TP's every weekend. I figure most people don't even know who lives there.

JENNY. Can't wait till middle school is over.

EMILY. I can't wait for high school. So much better than middle school.

JENNY. And twice as big.

EMILY. Did you know that ninth graders, like in Virginia(?), actually go to the high school?

JENNY. No fair! Only in backwards cackalacky. Bet that's Ol' Sperm Thurmond's fault.

EMILY. *(Thick Southern accent.)* Yes ma'am!

JENNY. Even in high school, there'll still be preps and jocks and heads.

EMILY. Maybe it'll change –

JENNY. I can't wait for summer.

EMILY. One month and twenty-one days to go.

JENNY. Ugh. That's for-ev-er. Can't wait for my birthday!

EMILY. In just twenty-nine days, you are going to be fifteen!

JENNY. I know. I don't really want to get older? I mean, I want to get out of middle school and I really want it to be summer and I'm excited to have a birthday party but getting older? I don't know –

EMILY. I know what you mean. Like, sometimes I think, we'll never ever be younger.

JENNY. This morning I looked in the mirror and thought: this is it. It's never going to get better than this.

EMILY. Really?

JENNY. Bet that's why John Pains tried to drive his car off the dam?

EMILY. He said, he said he did it for me. We never even kissed.

JENNY. You did wear his letter jacket.

EMILY. I was cold!

JENNY. No wonder his brother TP'ed your house.

EMILY. But Brian and I have Carolina history, fifth period, we sit together. He's my friend – I think.

>   *(Tiny pause.)*

JENNY. You know sometimes I lie down in my driveway and I let the fire ants bite my arm.

EMILY. That is totally sick.

JENNY. Really?

EMILY. I wouldn't do that. What movie should we watch first?

JENNY. *(British accent.)* I don't know darling. I can't decide. They all look so very, very rad.

EMILY. *(British accent.)* I'm frankly quite terrified of all of them.

JENNY. *(British accent.)* Well let's see – let's watch *Bloody Birthday*.

EMILY. I told you I saw it. This girl gets shot in the eye with an arrow – by her brother. It's gross.

JENNY. Cool.

>   *(**JENNY** puts Bloody Birthday in the tape player.)*

Hey! How's the play?

EMILY. I'm a dead person.

JENNY. I know. So?

EMILY. I only have four lines. We have a performance on your birthday.

JENNY. Really?

EMILY. Yeah (Sorry.) we do like, three. Will you come?

JENNY. Totally. So you like it?

EMILY. I like being the only middle schooler rehearsing a high school play.

JENNY. How is Adam Kennedy?

EMILY. He's missed the last two weeks.

JENNY. Did you read his poem in the literary magazine?

EMILY. Which one?

JENNY. The one about sex.

EMILY. Yup.

JENNY. Group sex. Orgy sex.

EMILY. The one titled: 'Proximal-Distal.'

JENNY. The hell does that mean?

EMILY. I think he's sayin' women's privates are proximal – like nearer to the volcanic? – center? – of a body? – and men's privates are distal and so farther from the center or 'point of attachment'? And he's using 'point of attachment' to mean like, two things...

JENNY. You are a total nerd.

EMILY. I know! I thought it was a good poem.

JENNY I heard he won some scholarship-thing.

EMILY. Really? My mom says he's an iconoclast. She said he's 'dangerous.'

JENNY. So where's he been?

EMILY. I don't know. I heard something about – like – a recovery center?

JENNY. No way.

EMILY. Yes huh.

JENNY. Heavy.

EMILY. Yeah.

JENNY. Is anyone else cool?

EMILY. Not really – I don't know? – They're all high-schoolers. I just sit and listen. This girl Sal has been giving me rides home and the other night she played me this song. Do you know Pink Floyd? 'Wish You Were Here.' I borrowed the mixed tape from her.

> (**EMILY** *gets up and searches in her bag for her walkman. She brings it to* **JENNY** *and rewinds until she finds the start of the song.*

JENNY *listens on the headphones. Note: The audience does not hear the song.)*

JENNY. Cool.

EMILY. Yeah.

JENNY. There's something about a song.

EMILY. Yeah.

JENNY. No – I mean – really something – you can just leave – wherever, the room – you know?

EMILY. Yeah.

JENNY. I like it.

EMILY. She has a lot of good music – Sal– she said this was 'retro' and she's not really into it anymore. She has a tattoo. She's a junior. She said she goes downtown, into Columbia, to concerts all the time and she knows some guys in bands –

JENNY. What's wrong with our music?

EMILY. Nothing. It's just she doesn't really listen to the radio – to Top 40 – you know?

JENNY. I like Top 40.

EMILY. (I know.) Me too – and she's a vegetarian. I'm thinking about doing it too. I hate my mom's meatloaf.

JENNY. But you have leather shoes. And letter jacket sleeves are leather. How could you wear a guy's letter jacket and be a vegetarian?

EMILY. Yeah. I haven't decided yet. That's a good point.

JENNY. Don't get all Birkenstock-granola-gross.

EMILY. I won't – but – do you know what gelatin is?

JENNY. Nope.

EMILY. Crushed up bits of animal bones – all the stuff they don't use for meat. Gross right? You know what gelatin is *in*?

JENNY. What?

EMILY. Skittles!

JENNY. No! I love Skittles.

EMILY. Me too! No more Skittles!

JENNY. I'm still gonna eat them.

(**EMILY** *looks at the Pringles label.*)

JENNY. Truth or Dare?

EMILY. Truth.

JENNY. Who do you most want to kiss?

EMILY. Adam Kennedy.

JENNY. Really? He's so funny-looking –

EMILY. Truth or Dare?

JENNY. Dare.

EMILY. Uhhh, I can't think of one.

JENNY. Come on. It can be dirty.

EMILY. I dare you to lick the tv.

JENNY. That is so lame!

EMILY. Well...

(**JENNY** *gets up and licks the tv.*)

JENNY. There. Happy?

EMILY. I don't know.

JENNY. Truth or Dare?

EMILY. Truth.

JENNY. You are such a nerd. Okay. Who do you want to lose it to?

EMILY. Adam Kennedy.

JENNY. Oh my god. You are so in love.

EMILY. I know.

JENNY. *(Serious.)* Really?

EMILY. I can't stop thinking about him. I sit up all night and write –

JENNY. Poetry?

EMILY. Kind of. No rhymes though. More like stream of consciousness and I listen to music –

JENNY. *(Lightly mocking.)* Candles and incense?

EMILY. Yes! I burn those candles we got in downtown – Columbia – remember? – the ones with the ocean and the unicorns? –

JENNY. Hey! – Forgot to tell you – my dad's having a party for like, my whole church? – Want to spend the night?

EMILY. When?

JENNY. Next weekend. Saturday night.

EMILY. Yes. Okay. So – let me tell you – I burn candles and I...think about what it would be like if he liked me.

JENNY. If he knew you were alive you mean?

EMILY. Yeah. He definitely looked at me the couple days he was at play practice. He made eye contact. He was kind of staring actually.

JENNY. He's out of our league.

EMILY. Maybe.

JENNY. Not maybe. For sure.

EMILY. I thought if I pretended to be sick he might want to take care of me.

JENNY. What? What the hell?

EMILY. Don't you think it might work?

JENNY. No way. Boys don't want to take care of you; they want S. E. X. Do you even know what happens when a boy has sex and...

EMILY. And what?

JENNY. Seriously?

EMILY. A little death?

JENNY. *(Laughing.)* No. What the hell? No – orgasm. Or it's called *(Mispronouncing 'cum.')* qume.

EMILY. I know that! I thought you were asking on a metaphorical level...forget it... Who told you?

JENNY. Angela Martin. In the bathroom between third and forth. She would know.

EMILY. She would.

JENNY. She said it tastes like –

EMILY. Tastes?!?!

JENNY. Yeah. What? You didn't know that part, huh?

EMILY. I don't know – I don't want to taste –

JENNY. Not even Adam Kennedy?

EMILY. Shut up.

JENNY. She said it tastes like bleach and banana and Hawaiian Tropic.

EMILY. *(Laughing.)* Oh my god.

   (**EMILY** *and* **JENNY** *collapse laughing.)*

JENNY. What is it about him?

EMILY. Adam?

JENNY. Yeah, Adam. He's not like Bubba or Dick or Kevin or any of the fine boys.

EMILY. I know. Maybe that's just it? He's smart. He's tall. He's old, he's like an adult.

JENNY. He's seventeen.

EMILY. He glows.

JENNY. Shut up.

EMILY. No – come on – you know what I mean. He glows, like he's special, he's going to do something in life. Sal told me that one time he, Adam, walked into class and someone had drawn a picture of the world on the chalk board and written his initials, A. R. K., in the middle and the names of all the girls in love with him orbiting the globe. And when Adam sat down everyone got real quiet and he got up – real slow – and just walked up there and erased it.

JENNY. And how does Sal know this?

EMILY. I think she's one of the girls in love with him. She told me she thinks his eyes are 'kaleidoscopes in the dark.'

JENNY. *(Laughing.)* Barf.

EMILY. I know. How could you even see a kaleidoscope in the dark?

JENNY. Double barf. He's in another league Emily, he has talents. He's good at things. He's going to have a life. Maybe he'll even be famous.

EMILY. Never underestimate a good listener.

   (Tiny, tiny pause.)

JENNY. What?

EMILY. Who do you want to lose it to?

JENNY. No one in town.

EMILY. Really?

JENNY. No way.

EMILY. Why?

JENNY. Losers.

EMILY. This whole town? But you think Bubba is hot – and he did give you kissing lessons –

JENNY. You don't know. You didn't grow up here. I've known everyone for-ev-er. So boring. Time is wasting!

EMILY. I think that would be nice.

JENNY. What?

EMILY. To know people forever.

JENNY. Why?

EMILY. I don't know – to get older with people that know you?

JENNY. Eww. Like who would you want to even see you old?

EMILY. You.

JENNY. Awwwwww shucks.

EMILY. Really.

JENNY. I want stuff to happen now. I'm bored of this town: all the lame boys.

EMILY. Why is it always boys?

JENNY. What?

EMILY. All day long, in class, I'm thinkin': Adam-Adam-Adam-Adam-Adam-Adam-Adam-

(**JENNY** *hits her with a pillow.*)

JENNY. I know!!

EMILY. And then, trying to do homework: Adam-Adam-Adam-Adam-

JENNY. I know!

(**JENNY** *hits her again. They laugh.*)

EMILY. Okay okay. Truth or Dare?

JENNY. Truth.

EMILY. Ha! Tell me something you've never said out loud to anyone before. Something true!

JENNY. Yikes. Okay. Okay – Sometimes when I'm in class and I'm bored or I'm just thinking I wish with all my heart that the classroom door would open and someone – someone famous – or someone like a discoverer-person – uh – a *Star-Search*-person – would come in and say to the teacher – in a whisper...'I'm here for Jenny.' And everyone – the whole class – would just turn and look at me and all the strut girls and Kevin and Bubba and they would all just wonder (??)...and I would stand up and walk out of class.

> *(Tiny pause.)*

EMILY. Then what?

JENNY. What?

EMILY. What happens? Are you famous? What do they want you for?

JENNY. Oh. I don't know.

EMILY. Well what happens next?

JENNY. I don't know. Does it matter?

EMILY. I think it does.

JENNY. Shut up.

EMILY. Think about it. What happens after?

JENNY. It's *my* dream.

EMILY. I know. I just – I feel that too *but* –

JENNY. Really?

EMILY. Yeah.

JENNY. *But??*

EMILY. Nothing – never mind –

> *(**JENNY** laughs.)*

JENNY. Okay movie time.

EMILY. Yes. But not *Bloody Birthday*.

JENNY. Fine. Which one do you want to watch?

EMILY. The dead cheerleader one.

JENNY. Okay. But it is my house I should get to pick.

EMILY. We're always at your house. You always get to pick.

JENNY. Fine.

> (**JENNY** *ejects* Bloody Birthday *and puts* Dead Cheerleader Camp *in the video player. The girls get comfortable on the bed – close enough to touch.)*
>
> *(Beat.)*

Jenny and Joseph: Scene 1

(A little under a month later, toward the end of May. A converted sunken living room in a suburban home. A couch, a tv, bookshelves, sliding glass doors to a backyard, upstage a full bathroom, stairs going up, and a door that leads to the garage.)

JOSEPH. So – this is my place.

JENNY. It's real nice.

JOSEPH. Do you want anything to drink? I have everything –

JENNY. Do you have Diet Coke?

JOSEPH. Yup.

> *(**JOSEPH** goes out and comes back with a Diet Coke.)*

JENNY. Thank you!

JOSEPH. Welcome.

> *(**JENNY** licks the entire top of the can and then pops it open and takes a big drink.)*

JENNY. So what music do you like?

JOSEPH. To listen to?

JENNY. Yah. To listen to.

JOSEPH. Uh. I like Journey and Billy Idol. I love Hall & Oates!...and Pink Floyd –

JENNY. Oh!! I think I've heard Pink Floyd – it's like, 'retro'?

JOSEPH. Yeah. I guess it is. Which album?

JENNY. Uh...crap...Uh...

JOSEPH. ...Or song?

JENNY. I don't remember... I wish I did...??

JOSEPH. Most of their stuff is good. Real silky – cool.

JENNY. Oh. Uh-huh.

JOSEPH. Here. I'll play something –

(He goes to the bookshelf and puts a tape in the tape player.)*

Come sit down –

(Tiny pause. She sits next to him on the couch.)

JENNY. I thought you looked like Tom Cruise.

JOSEPH. What?

(He gets up and turns the music down a little. Comes back and sits next to her.)

JENNY. When I saw you – the first time. I thought you looked just like Tom Cruise.

JOSEPH. *(He smiles big/toothy.)* Oh yeah? *Top Gun* was great.

JENNY. Yah(!)…Who do you think I look like?

JOSEPH. What?

JENNY. Do you think I look like someone famous? Everyone does – you know – I mean everyone *secretly* thinks they look just like someone famous – like they look in the mirror to do lipstick or whatever and they think: *Oh yeah, Brooke Shields, oh yeah*…or whatever. So?

JOSEPH. You look just like yourself. Just like – you.

JENNY. I totally would have gone away with you right then. If you had asked…

JOSEPH. What?

JENNY. The first time I saw you – at Dad's church party –

JOSEPH. Really? At night? With me? A stranger?

JENNY. Okay so maybe the second time? – That was afternoon not night – outside school – remember??

JOSEPH. You were eating Twizzlers.

---

*A license to produce *All the Fine Boys* does not include a performance license for any third-party or copyrighted music. Licensees should create an original composition or use music in the public domain. For further information, please see Music Use Note on page 3.

JENNY. Yah. I love Twizzlers! You aren't a stranger. You go to my church, you were at my house.

JOSEPH. You don't know me.

JENNY. Yes I do!

JOSEPH. Do you?

JENNY. Oh yeah sure. Let's see. Your name is Joe. You like to drive fast and listen to rock bands I never heard of. You have a real nice car –

JOSEPH. It's a Miata –

JENNY. – *And* a nice house. You hold doors open. You're no stranger. 'Sides you're too good-lookin' to be bad.

JOSEPH. *(Smiling again.)* Am I now? Am I good-lookin'?

JENNY. Yup.

JOSEPH. You know, I saw *you* before your dad's party.

JENNY. You did?

JOSEPH. Yeah. At church.

JENNY. *(Flattered.)* Oh.

JOSEPH. You know what else you don't know?

JENNY. *(Giggling.)* No...

JOSEPH. I used to ride a motorcycle.

JENNY. *(Very excited.)* Oh my god – No way! Like *Top Gun*! I never met anyone who rode a motorcycle before. Why'd you stop?

JOSEPH. I had a pretty good accident.

JENNY. I'd love to ride on a motorcycle. I mean, I love my bike, and I can imagine –

JOSEPH. Oh yeah. You feel very alive but also very, very close to – well, to death. Not like you think that – I mean, you just think about the road and the wind is so loud it's kind of peaceful.

JENNY. I'd love to try it.

JOSEPH. Maybe you'll get to one day.

JENNY. With you?

JOSEPH. Yeah.

(They smile at each other.)

I'm also a champion skeet shooter.

JENNY. Wow! That's so cool.

JOSEPH. Do you shoot skeet?

JENNY. Um-no-sorry- (What is it?)

JOSEPH. Okay so you take your shotgun and go the range and shoot clay pigeons. I belong to Shooters Choice Gun Club in Wes' Columbia. You know it?

> (**JENNY** *shakes her head 'no.'*)

– Shootin' skeets is real hard, real challenging. Want to see my trophy?

JENNY. Yeah!

> (*He goes to the bookcase and takes down a large skeet shooting trophy. He hands it to her.*)

JOSEPH. This was a tough win. Best In State. It's an Olympic event you know?

JENNY. Oh – Are you – ? Olympic?!

JOSEPH. Nah. I'm pretty famous 'round here though – folks know – maybe one day.

JENNY. Wow.

JOSEPH. Yeah. I go to competitions a lot. I'm real competitive.

JENNY. Wow.

> (**JOSEPH** *smiles.*)
>
> (*Tiny pause.*)

JOSEPH. What's your favorite thing for dinner?

JENNY. (*Trying to get away with something.*) Pizza. And and – Pringles. But only in the red cans. Cheese puffs – not Cheetos – puffs...the kind with the air blown in. Oreos. Twizzlers. Peppermint Patties. Moon Pies! Blow Pops. Big League Chew bubble gum. Candy apples – the car-mel kind, but mostly only at the Okra Strut. Pringles are my favorite.

JOSEPH. (*Smiling.*) That's dinner?

JENNY. Totally.

JOSEPH. I think I have some of those things here. We could have that for dinner.

JENNY. Really??

   (Pause.)

   I'm hungry.

JOSEPH. Already?

JENNY. I always eat when I get home from school.

JOSEPH. What's the Okra Strut like?

JENNY. You have got to be kidding!

JOSEPH. Nope. Never been –

JENNY. Wow. Do you like, lock – the – doors and stay inside all fall?

JOSEPH. Naw – I go to the Clemson/Carolina games. Tell me about it?

JENNY. It's a parade for a vegetable. An okra queen, an okra-eating contest. Southern Strut dances in the high school parking lot – they're *real* good – but most of those girls are stuck-up. They were on *Star Search*. They have floats and rides. It's like a fair. And, at night, they have a dance in the Kroger parking lot. Loud music. Lights on strings.

JOSEPH. Sounds nice.

JENNY. It is. It's real nice (for a tiny town).

JOSEPH. I like rides. I like roller coasters.

JENNY. Me too! I like fairs *so* much. And how happy everyone is – just walking around. And the smell –

JOSEPH. Fair smell? Pigs?

JENNY. No! Cotton candy. Pretzels and sausage and –

JOSEPH. Okra?

JENNY. *(Squishing up her face.)* Fried okra is so gross. Seriously. It's still slimy.

JOSEPH. I'd like to go. I'll even try the fried okra.

JENNY. I'll take you –

JOSEPH. That would be nice.

JENNY. It's the biggest parade in the state.

JOSEPH. Really?

JENNY. Yah.

(*Tiny beat.*)

I think I know what's going to happen with us, don't you?

JOSEPH. ...Do you?

JENNY. Well...

JOSEPH. (*Very direct.*) What do you think is going to happen?

JENNY. (*Giggling, blushing.*) Never mind...

JOSEPH. Uh-huh.

JENNY. I'm hungry.

JOSEPH. Well then. I'll go get –

JENNY. Can I come? Can I see the rest of the house?

JOSEPH. No stay here – I want to surprise you.

JENNY. Please...

JOSEPH. Don't you like surprises?

JENNY. Yeah...

JOSEPH. Wait here.

JENNY. (*Saluting.*) Okay. Yes sir!

JOSEPH. Back in a jiffy –

(**JOSEPH** *leaves up the stairs.* **JENNY** *picks up the phone and dials.*)

JENNY. Hey Mrs. Wilson it's Jennifer may I please speak with Emily? Thank you...

(**JENNY** *twirls the phone cord around her foot, her leg, her arm. As she talks, she wanders around the room looking at stuff – opening drawers, looking at the bookcase.*)

Hey... John Pains is getting married! ...I know. And on the same day he graduates too! ...

(*She finds a Bible.*)

JENNY. Aw fuck! *(What-no-not you! – I was just – never mind.)* – In sixth period...hey – don't wear those shorts again...nope... Bye.

    (She hangs up the phone.)

    (Beat.)

Adam and Emily: Scene A

(A suburban rec room over a garage. The same day in May. The ceiling starts low and is slanted up into a triangle. There is a small window on the far wall, the room is carpeted, and the walls are covered in political stickers and band stickers/posters. Many 'Shut down the River Plant' signs taped to the wall. Clear signs of inhabitance by high school boys with permissive parents. A guitar, an amp. A huge tv – late 1970s model; an old couch facing the tv. ADAM sits on the couch. He is working on his part in the school play or playing his guitar or composing a poem – earnestly.)

(EMILY knocks on the door. ADAM gets up and opens the door, stands holding it wide.)

ADAM. Well hello ma'am.

EMILY. Hey. I was on my bike. Your dad said I could just come up?

ADAM. Cool. So?

EMILY. So?

ADAM. You seem to have recovered from your mysterious illness.

EMILY. Oh. Yes – oh – yes.

ADAM. And you got my possibly-diagnostic letter?

EMILY. You drew the directions to your house?

> *(EMILY opens her fist to reveal a folded piece of notebook paper – it's kind of smashed and well-loved, read over and over.)*

ADAM. Ah yes.

EMILY. And told me to come over? So I came over?

ADAM. Come in – sit down... Middle school: seventh, eighth and ninth grade, is almost a complete mixture of greatness and hell, you know?

EMILY. Yeah. (?)

ADAM. When I was in middle school the great part was screwing around a lot and getting out of school a lot and geezing the administrators because we were smarter than them. We did the Pops Concert which kicked.

> (**ADAM** *gets up and plays the guitar idly.*)

EMILY. They still have that.

ADAM. They do?

EMILY. Yeah – Pops!

ADAM. Cool. Our legacy. Also, middle school sucks. Everybody (except for about ten people) hated me and my friends and threw rocks at us and spit on us and beat us up.

EMILY. Really? Why?

ADAM. Dunno. I was in love with a black girl. I had purple hair. Do the haters need a reason why? Anyways, out of all that I rose up to become the terrific guy you see today.

> (**ADAM** *grins at* **EMILY.** *She grins back.*)

You should enjoy middle school while you can but high school is a lot better.

EMILY. I can't wait.

ADAM. Well, ma'am, I asked you here to tell you this: whenever us guys in the show pick on you about being in middle school we're just kidding.

EMILY. Okay. I know. I guess.

ADAM. Some of us still wish we were there, and some of us are just sad you're not old enough for us to date.

EMILY. Oooo!

> (**EMILY** *is stricken.* **ADAM** *misses the look as he sets the guitar aside. He turns around.*)

ADAM. Are you okay?

EMILY. I don't feel well.

ADAM. What's wrong?

EMILY. I'm having trouble breathing.

ADAM. Again?

EMILY. *(Panting, labored breath.)* Uh-huh

ADAM. Can I do anything to help?

EMILY. I – uh – don't – uh – think – uh – so.

> (**ADAM** *turns* **EMILY** *to him. He looks at her. Intensely. He puts both hands on her face, one on either cheek, cupping her jaw.)*

ADAM. You are very beautiful.

EMILY. *(Wincing, smiling.)* No I'm not.

ADAM. Well, I have been known to have strange taste.

EMILY. Is it true you were sent – went – away?

> (**ADAM** *gets up.)*

ADAM. Where'd you hear that?

EMILY. I overheard – girls – at play practice and you weren't there for, like, two weeks –

ADAM. Yeah, my parents freaked out about the music I was into and I was drinking so – they sent me away for a couple weeks. Dad's a psychiatrist, Mom's a psychologist not great for dealing with us kids, you know?

EMILY. But you're okay?

ADAM. I was sitting looking out the window – this was real early in the a.m. and – this is when I was 'in' – and I was wearing these striped pajamas and I heard this song – Do you know the Smiths?

> (**ADAM** *gets up and plays* **EMILY** *a fast, bright song.)**

I heard that and I knew I was going to be fine. A-okay. Okey-dokey.

EMILY. I've never heard The Smiths.

ADAM. You should. They kick.

---

*A license to produce *All the Fine Boys* does not include a performance license for any third-party or copyrighted music. Licensees should create an original composition or use music in the public domain. For further information, please see Music Use Note on page 3.

(*Awkward silence.* **ADAM** *kind of walks around the room.*)

EMILY. Did you know that guy that drowned in Lake Murray?

ADAM. Yeah. He was a friend.

EMILY. Is it true his Docs filled with water and he couldn't get them off?

ADAM. Yup. He always wore ten-hole.

EMILY. Did you know the girl that went off the dam?

ADAM. Nope.

EMILY. I don't think she jumped. I think she fell.

ADAM. You think?

EMILY. She was pretty; she worked at Spinnakers in the mall.

ADAM. Did you know the kids that were in the car that got hit by the train?

EMILY. Nope. But one of them – the girl – was in my mom's class. You know she's a teacher at the high school. She knows who you are –

ADAM. Is that a good thing?

EMILY. Probably not but she does like that you edit the literary magazine.

ADAM. (*Laughing.*) Alright.

EMILY. Anyway, she said, my mom said, the girl in her class, she said she was a real overachiever. A real pity – she said.

ADAM. I knew the driver. He was my year. I wonder how that happened all the time...

EMILY. The last place I lived, no one ever died.

ADAM. Where was that?

EMILY. Virginia.

ADAM. Maybe they're dying there now.

EMILY. Yeah. Maybe.

ADAM. When did you move here?

EMILY. Um, a year ago, last summer. So almost two years ago – now – We move a lot. My family –

ADAM. That must be nice.

EMILY. Sometimes it is.

ADAM. *(Bitterly rueful.)* I figure staying in one place, it allows you to be lazy, you know? You don't have to define your culture or individualism or fight to be known 'cause everybody remembers you playing kickball and shit. You *can't* change. Might be nice to swap towns.

EMILY. I always think, each time we move, I think, in the new place I'll go by a new name and I'll be – I don't know – different? But it never happens –

ADAM. Why not?

EMILY. I don't know. If I changed my name would I still be me? Being known real well sounds nice to me.

ADAM. Nah. Lazy – but that's my suburban malaise talkin'.

EMILY. I'd like to be someone who has really old friends, hometown-friends that have known me since, like, forever? You know?

ADAM. Yah – I don't. Recently, there has been a big outcry by all my old friends about my arrogance.

EMILY. Are you arrogant?

ADAM. This is what I think: my arrogance seems really terrible to them because of its contrast to their insecurity which is by anyone's definition *really* really terrible.

EMILY. So, you aren't friends anymore?

ADAM. I haven't decided yet.

EMILY. When I moved, I lost all my old friends. There was this group of us girls. Five of us. We always hung out, spend-the-nights and stuff. When I moved here, that first summer I wrote them all letters and I tried to make this place sound real good. You know? Like I was having a good time and there are palm trees here and I go swimming every day and one by one they stopped writing me back, I didn't hear from anyone – and then, I got this group letter and they all signed it and it said: 'You like it so much better there, good, have a nice life we never liked you anyway.'

ADAM. That's rough.

EMILY. Yeah. 'An outcry' I guess? But see, I was lying. I was miserable here – just sitting in my house reading. Missing them. Lonely.

ADAM. But that's much cooler. Your mistake was not being honest about your grief.

EMILY. Really? I mean – I think that *pretending* to be happy – or brave? – is being a good friend...you know? Better then complaining –

ADAM. Did you write back?

EMILY. I did. I was real mad. It took me a long time. I wrote, like, a tome.

ADAM. What happened?

EMILY. I didn't send it.

ADAM. Why not?

EMILY. My dad said don't. Turn the other cheek.

ADAM. I wish I had more time; I've gotta go downtown to see my lady-friend.

EMILY. Oh! Okay.

ADAM. Please ma'am if you would, make me a glorious list of items.

EMILY. What?

ADAM. You know, write down a list of glorious things and give it to me.

EMILY. Oh okay.

ADAM. I can drive you home if you like. We can put your bike in my bus. My girl, she lives downtown, in Columbia.

EMILY. Does she go to a different school?

ADAM. Yeah. USC. She's a senior.

EMILY. *(Swallowing.)* Wow!!

ADAM. Tonight is adult night. We dress up and pretend we are adults and we make up shit to talk about like 'the kids' and 'the bills' and sometimes we have huge fights about 'renovations to the house.' Mostly we have sex and she drinks red wine. She's cool. You'd like her.

EMILY. Are you, are you serious about her? I mean – are you thinking of –

ADAM. What's it to you??

EMILY. *(Turning red.)* Ah –

ADAM. I'm kidding. It's cool – I mean – *we're* here together now. Right?

EMILY. Right?

ADAM. If patterns are repeated, they mean things.

EMILY. And that's okay with her?

ADAM. Yeah. It's okay.

> (**ADAM** *opens the door for* **EMILY.** *She walks out and down the stairs. He follows her out, shutting the door behind them.)*
>
> *(Beat.)*

Jenny and Joseph: Scene 1.5

(The same day. **JOSEPH** *returns down the stairs with an armful of candy [Twizzlers] and cans of Pringles.)*

JOSEPH. Look what I found –

*(***JENNY*** *opens a large red can of Pringles and eats chips.)*

JENNY. Oh my – Thank you thank you thank you.

JOSEPH. Happy?

JENNY. Yes!

(She's eating.)

JOSEPH. Skeet's the great American shotgun game. It's one of the greatest sports America invented.

JENNY. *(Not really interested.)* Oh yeah?

JOSEPH. Yeah. 'Sides football. Olympic skeet has much faster targets than regular.

(She's eating.)

JENNY. Oh.

JOSEPH. *(Holding an imagined gun on his hip.)* Yah – you have ta'start with the gun like so –

(He looks at her. She's eating. Tiny pause.)

Hey. Want to watch a movie?

JENNY. Yes!

JOSEPH. What kind of movies do you like?

JENNY. My friend Emily and I mostly watch horror movies. In – in – *her* basement.

JOSEPH. What's your favorite?

JENNY. *The Serpent and the Rainbow.*

JOSEPH. Aren't you a little young to watch that?

JENNY. *(A lie – it's her basement.) Emily's* mom rents them for us. We watch them in *her* basement on this bed that's down there with lots of pillows and blankets.

It's cold down there even in summer. Her mom? She totally rents us like, anything.

JOSEPH. What about your mom?

JENNY. She doesn't know about the movies –

JOSEPH. Would she let you have this dinner?

JENNY. *(A truth.)* No. Total health freak. Apples and bran muffins.

JOSEPH. Really?

> *(Tiny pause.)*

JENNY. Oh yeah.

JOSEPH. Well don't tell her.

JENNY. I totally won't. [I used to ride my bike to the gas station and just like s... – um, like used my allowance – to like – buy candy bars and then eat them all on the bike ride home. And one time I totally told my mom this big story about how I hate malted milk balls but the whole time I had this giant box of malted milk balls in my underwear drawer.

JOSEPH. Why?

JENNY. Why what?

JOSEPH. Why would you do that?

JENNY. Oh. I don't know? I totally got caught. She like did laundry and like put my underwear away all neat and was like, 'I thought you told me you hate malted milk balls...' You know?

JOSEPH. Uh-huh.]

> *([ ] Indicate possible cut.)*

JENNY. Candy is like total contraband – Thank you thank you thank you! These are really good Pringles. Fresh. It's not that they go bad, it's that some cans are just better. This is a good can.

JOSEPH. Good. I'm glad.

> *(**JENNY** eats more Pringles. **JOSEPH** gets up to adjust the music. Tiny pause.)*

JENNY. Have you ever traveled?

JOSEPH. What do you mean? Where?

JENNY. Anywhere.

JOSEPH. Well. I've been to Utah. And I rode my motorcycle along the California coast once. And I went to Hawaii.

JENNY. Wow. Really? Hawaii. I'd like to go there. Tell me about it?

(He sits back down.)

JOSEPH. It's nice. Very, nice sand, very tropical. The traffic to and from the airport was real bad. You wouldn't think it would be but it was. The whole island: bumper-to-bumper traffic. But the beach is nice. It's not as relaxing as you would think. The whole piña colada culture s'not for me. There's a lot of pressure to relax which isn't very relaxing.

JENNY. Still – it'ould be something to go to Hawaii – better than first week at ol' Myrtle Beach.

JOSEPH. Well, maybe you'll go one day. I travel a lot for the skeet too. Mostly in-state but also to Georgia. And Texas. The National Association is in Texas. And one time to Chino. That's where they had the Olympics in '84.

JENNY. I always wanted to go to Georgia.

JOSEPH. Oh yeah?

JENNY. Yeah. There's a boy at the high school who does Olympic rowing.

JOSEPH. Really?

JENNY. Yeah.

JOSEPH. What's his name?

JENNY. Chris Benson.

JOSEPH. Never heard a'him.

JENNY. I don't know him. He's at the high school.

(Tiny pause.)

JOSEPH. It's nice for you to want to go places, you know, when you're young, to dream about places to travel to... something to look forward to.

JENNY. In all my dreams –

JOSEPH. What?

JENNY. Never mind.

JOSEPH. What?

JENNY. Nah...

JOSEPH. Tell me. I'm interested.

JENNY. Well, like, I know the world is really big, you know? no duh. And I get that, like, *I'm not* – like compared to the whole world or...you know? But in my dreams, I'm – so – much more?

JOSEPH. Like you're ten feet tall?

JENNY. Yes!

JOSEPH. I know what you mean. I feel that way too.

JENNY. You do?

JOSEPH. Yeah.

> *(They smile at each other.)*

JENNY. I never – like – told anyone any of this –

JOSEPH. You mean your goals?

JENNY. Yeah.

JOSEPH. Why not?

JENNY. No one asks? My daddy says girls are easy to raise: 'You just love 'em and expect nothin' from 'em' –

> *(**JOSEPH** laughs. **JENNY** laughs too.)*

JOSEPH. Hey! I love this song.

> *(He jumps up and turns the volume up.)*

Want to dance?

JENNY. What?

> *(He holds out his hand.)*

JOSEPH. Dance with me?

> *(She gets up and dances a little. He dances too. Then he pulls her in to dance with him. It's a little awkward, but sweet. She laughs and whispers in his ear.)*

JENNY. I'm planning a trip.

JOSEPH. Where?

JENNY. Promise not to tell?

JOSEPH. Yes.

JENNY. I don't know – exactly? – I mean I have a lot of ideas; I have a notebook full of places that look nice in movies and on tv and places I've heard about –

JOSEPH. Are you going by yourself?

> *(They are standing very close. She's nervous and starts talking fast:)*

JENNY. Maybe. Maybe not. Depends. I'd like Emily to come with me but she's really into this boy. Everyone is into him but not in a football way –

JOSEPH. A road trip?

JENNY. Duh. Don't have money for a plane do I? Emily went on a plane once. She went on this Junior Scholars trip. I was crazy jealous of that. Not the scholar thing that's for nerds but the plane thing. That's cool. Don't tell her.

JOSEPH. Okay. Jenny?

JENNY. – 'Course I need to get my learner's permit which my folks promised me I can try-for after my birthday –

JOSEPH. Jenny?

JENNY. Yeah? I've – been studyin' for the test – its real soon – this weekend.

JOSEPH. *(Touching her face.)* You're a very pretty girl.

JENNY. *(Lighting up.)* ...You think so?

JOSEPH. ...Don't you hear that all the time?

JENNY. *(A lie.)* Oh yeah. All the time.

> *(They kiss.)*

JOSEPH. I really like you Jenny.

JENNY. I like you too –

> *(He has his hand on the back of her head.)*

JOSEPH. I can't believe you're... – your hair is so soft –

JENNY. Joe.

> *(They kiss again.)*

> *(Stopping him.)* Want to watch a movie?

JOSEPH. Okay.

> *(***JOSEPH*** puts a video in the player.)*

> *(Beat.)*

Adam and Emily: Scene B

*(The next day. **ADAM** and **EMILY** in the rec room. Evening. A thunderstorm outside.)*

ADAM. Where does your mom think you are?

EMILY. Play practice.

ADAM. Doesn't she know how late it goes?

EMILY. I'm not sure.

ADAM. That's a dangerous game young lady.

EMILY. So?

ADAM. Did you make me a glorious list.

EMILY. Yes.

ADAM. Read it to me.

*(**EMILY** opens her backpack and takes out a notebook. She reads:)*

EMILY. Great beauty, magnificent adoration, praise, thanksgiving, worship, the splendor and bliss of heaven, perfect happiness, a halo, nimbus or aureole.

ADAM. That's not a list. That's the dictionary definition.

EMILY. Oh, uh, so, okay... God, dying for love, war, flying, the ocean –

ADAM. That's BIG stuff.

EMILY. ??

ADAM. Gothic-type romantic stuff.

EMILY. ...

ADAM. And abstracts. You seem to like the abstracts.

EMILY. What's wrong with romance and the ocean?

ADAM. Think about stuff like: pears, zithers, pigs, fingernails, thermometers, a whole bunch of sweaty kids all dancing in a small room, light-bulbs... You get the idea.

EMILY. Is that stuff really glorious? Filled with glory?

ADAM. There are no small things, Emily.

EMILY. ...

ADAM. Did you know that birds have hollow bones?

EMILY. No – wait, what?

ADAM. There is a place I want to go with you – a bakery called Cribbs. It's very good. Very focused. They have real good cupcakes with plastic farm animals on top.

EMILY. I like cupcakes.

ADAM. Me too.

EMILY. Cupcakes are glorious.

ADAM. So are plastic farm animals.

> (**EMILY** *laughs.*)

I think Stacey and I broke up. We had sex on her kitchen table. It was good sex but break-up sex I think. I can still smell her on my hands.

EMILY. …

ADAM. I'm gonna miss her.

EMILY. …

ADAM. Do you know that smell?

> (**ADAM** *offers his hand to* **EMILY** *to smell.*)

Here.

> (**EMILY** *smells his hand.* **ADAM** *grins like a kid.*)

Is there somewhere you'd like to go? We can go anywhere.

EMILY. …

ADAM. Where do you go to be by yourself?

EMILY. This playground. It has good swings.

ADAM. We should go there.

EMILY. It's just a kids' playground.

ADAM. When I was little I was swinging on a swing set and I swung way out, horizontal and parallel to the ground and the chain busted and I felt the inertia pull me out, away from the swing and the plastic sliding out in front of me and my heart in my throat because I was falling but the worst thing was the sound when I landed. It wasn't my body hitting the ground, but another noise dull and sick and loud. It was the left chain popping a girl in the swing beside mine in the eye, and her eyelid opening up and then her screaming. I opened my mouth to do the same but couldn't because I couldn't breathe and she was bleeding and screaming and I struggled for breath and I felt guilty. Isn't that silly? I felt guilty about that.

EMILY. It wasn't your fault.

ADAM. I know... What are you thinking about?

EMILY. My friend Jenny.

ADAM. (Oh.)

EMILY. She cut school today. And I didn't hear from her and she calls me *every* day.

ADAM. The day's not done yet...

EMILY. Yeah –

ADAM. Sometimes that's a necessary crime.

EMILY. Skipping school?

ADAM. Yeah. I used to. The trick is how to get away with it –

EMILY. I'd never get away with it. My mom always knows where I am.

ADAM. But you are at play practice right now.

EMILY. *(Realizing!)* (Oh yeah!)

ADAM. Yeah. Disappearing is easy as a lie.

(**ADAM** *lights a smoke.*)

EMILY. My church has a cool basement.

ADAM. ???

EMILY. You said where do I like to go? Well, my church has this cool basement under the nave, you go down all these stone stairs, and it's always cold down there no matter how hot it is. It gets so hot here. Candles are piled everywhere, loads of books, racks of robes, old pews, tables piled with stuff.

ADAM. Sounds perfect.

EMILY. It's downtown. Trinity Cathedral. Do you know it?

ADAM. Yup. It survived Sherman's March. Oldest cemetery in the state. That's your church?

EMILY. It's cool right?

ADAM. You know how to get into the basement?

EMILY. *(Courageously flirting.)* I'm an acolyte.

ADAM. *(Teasingly.)* Wow.

EMILY. The first time I went down there I couldn't believe what a mess.

ADAM. Sounds glorious. Gothic and crap. Have you ever been to the river plant?

EMILY. Nope.

ADAM. They have a beautiful, quiet path by the river. Or it used to be – before the leak – (Goddamn that leak!) I haven't been in awhile.

> *(**ADAM** gets up and rummages in some boxes. He finds an old candle – burned low – nothing but a nub. He searches some more and finds a metal grain label and a magnet advertising the South Carolina Farm Bureau.)*

Here. Presents.

> *(**EMILY** stands up.)*

EMILY. For me?

ADAM. This is just an old candle.

EMILY. Did *you* burn it down?

ADAM. Yes, I did. This magnet's cool though.

> *(They are standing very close.)*

EMILY. *(On the metal tag.)* What's that?

ADAM. That's from when they used to label the cotton bales with metal tags. Got that off a farm.

> *(He looks down at her. **EMILY** laughs. She moves away and puts the 'presents' in her backpack.)*

If you want something to happen you have to make it happen.

EMILY. What?

ADAM. Initiate what you want to happen.

EMILY. I –

ADAM. Don't just wish.

EMILY. I – I'm not – idle –

ADAM. There are always risks but they are outweighed by
the possibilities. If you want to kiss me, you should.

> (**EMILY** *turns red, she looks away, he turns her
> face to his.*)

What could you lose? A little pride if I reject you? Too
much pride is damaging and I won't – anyway – and
you know that. Don't you?

EMILY. No.

> (**ADAM** *lets go of her face. They sit side by side
> on the couch.* **ADAM** *smokes his Lucky Strike.*)

But why? Why couldn't *you* just kiss *me*?

ADAM. That would be dangerous.

EMILY. Kissing?

ADAM. You're not very clear on our position, are you? I'm
not either. That's something for us to talk about.

EMILY. Okay. So –

ADAM. So. May I touch you?

EMILY. Yes.

> (**ADAM** *puts his hand on her face and very
> gently traces her forehead and cheeks and
> lips. [His hands smell like cigarettes and
> patchouli.] He stops and* **EMILY** *opens her
> eyes.*)

ADAM. I once told someone I would go blind for a week to
be able to kiss you.

EMILY. Uh um okay uh so... Who did you tell?

ADAM. Chris Benson.

EMILY. – The *Olympic* guy??

ADAM. May I?

EMILY. What?

ADAM. Kiss you Emily.

EMILY. Oh. Yes.

> *(They kiss. At first* **EMILY** *doesn't know what to do with her hands. Then she puts them around* **ADAM** *and hides her fingers in his hair. She smiles. They stop kissing and she laughs and he smiles too. He puts the Lucky back in his mouth.)*

ADAM. Let's go to the river plant.

EMILY. But it's dark out!

ADAM. You'll still be able to *see* –

EMILY. But it's raining!

ADAM. So??

EMILY. I think – I think I love you –

ADAM. *(Chuckling.)* Let's go kid.

> *(She is giddy, dancy, and jumpy as they leave the rec room. Beat.)*

Jenny and Joseph: Scene 2

*(The same day as Adam and Emily's previous scene – but much earlier, early morning. **JENNY**, fully dressed, asleep on the couch – heavy teenage sleep – sprawled out. **JOSEPH** enters. He stands over her and watches her for a minute. He is dressed very neatly in different clothes.)*

JOSEPH. Wake up....Jenny...wake up...

(He shakes her foot.)

JENNY. ...Oh...hi... I fell asleep?

JOSEPH. I couldn't wake you –

JENNY. What time is it?

JOSEPH. Morning.

JENNY. I can't believe I spent the night! Ha!

JOSEPH. We have to get you home.

JENNY. What time is it?

JOSEPH. Eight.

JENNY. School starts in like eighteen minutes.

JOSEPH. Then we have to get you to school.

JENNY. I don't want to go.

JOSEPH. Where do your parents think you are?

JENNY. I left a note – they won't worry.

JOSEPH. For how long?

JENNY. *(Lies.)* Awhile – I think. I said I was spending the night at Emily's – a couple nights – at Emily's... I do it all the time...

JOSEPH. Are you sure?

JENNY. *(A lie.)* They won't even notice –

(He opens the sliding glass door and walks outside. She watches him.)

*(**JENNY** takes a crumbled pack of cigarettes from her shorts pocket. She walks outside and lights one.)*

JOSEPH. You shouldn't smoke.

JENNY. You sound like my mom.

JOSEPH. Well. She's right. Smoking is disgustin'.

> *(He takes the cigarette from her, stamps it out, and paces a bit.)*

JENNY. Hey! I only have two.

> *(She takes out the second one.)*

JOSEPH. Where'd you get these?

> *(He takes the second one and grinds it out too.)*

JENNY. *(Shrugging.)* ???

JOSEPH. I don't want you smoking. You can't smoke here. Got it?

JENNY. *(Saluting.)* Okay!

JOSEPH. And you like junk food too much.

JENNY. Jesus...

JOSEPH. Don't take his name in vain –

JENNY. Oh-my-god – (Shit! Sorry.) – seriously?

JOSEPH. Yes. You should take vitamins.

> *(**JENNY** laughs.)*

JENNY. Do you need some coffee, Mr. Grumpy?

JOSEPH. I don't drink coffee. You should take better care of yourself.

JENNY. Okay Mom.

JOSEPH. It sounds like you have a very good, health-conscious mom.

JENNY. Not really.

JOSEPH. You shouldn't say that.

JENNY. Even if it's true?

JOSEPH. My mother is a saint.

JENNY. Oh I'm sorry – when did she die?

JOSEPH. She's not dead!

JENNY. But you just said –

JOSEPH. No.

JENNY. Wow.

JOSEPH. I'm not old if that's what you are implying.

JENNY. Yes you are – I'm sorry – you *so* are!

JOSEPH. I'm really not.

JENNY. How old?

JOSEPH. Twenty-eight.

JENNY. *(Laughing.)* That is sooo sooo ancient – I mean – you are old enough to like... I don't know? – You're old – like almost at my folks' age –

JOSEPH. I don't feel old.

JENNY. Did you go to college already?

JOSEPH. Yes.

JENNY. Old! Do you have a regular adult job?

JOSEPH. Yes.

JENNY. Old!! Do you get up on Sunday and go to church all by your lonesome?

JOSEPH. Every Sunday.

JENNY. Old!!! But it's okay 'cause you're foxy too...

(**JOSEPH** *smiles and laughs.*)

JOSEPH. I used to see you at church.

JENNY. You said.

JOSEPH. I used to watch you.

JENNY. Go Holy Cross!!

JOSEPH. Really.

JENNY. More than one time?

JOSEPH. Yes. How come you don't take communion?

JENNY. I didn't finish the classes. My dad takes it serious. Lots of kids just take communion without getting confirmed but not me.

JOSEPH. You should finish the classes.

JENNY. Yeah. It's just me and the little kids kneeling with our arms crossed getting blessings on our head. Makes me feel so dumb. Like, I'm way too old for the classes now anyway?

JOSEPH. Nah – you don't look dumb.

JENNY. Yeah right.

JOSEPH. I've seen you, remember?

JENNY. *(Counting off three on her fingers.)* I only remember seeing you: at Dad's party, outside school, and when you picked me up at my house.

JOSEPH. You don't go so often anymore.

JENNY. To church?

JOSEPH. Do you miss it?

JENNY. Church? Nah…maybe? Sometimes. I liked Bible stories – like – when I was a kid…

JOSEPH. You should start going again and get confirmed.

JENNY. Well if I get to see you there…

> *(Tiny pause.)*

So what do you do for your grown-up job?

JOSEPH. I work at the river plant.

JENNY. Doing what?

JOSEPH. I'm a nuclear technician – engineer. I'm a nuclear engineer.

JENNY. Wow-wow – you must make a ton of dough.

JOSEPH. *(Amused, pleased.)* I make enough. I do fine.

JENNY. Seriously. You must be so – so – smart.

JOSEPH. Well – yes.

JENNY. I can't believe this. Like how much?

JOSEPH. How much what?

JENNY. Dough. Bucks??

JOSEPH. That's private.

JENNY. *(Flirty.)* Come on, you can tell me…

JOSEPH. It's very bad manners to ask someone how much money they make. Really.

JENNY. I'm sorry.

JOSEPH. That's fine. Apology accepted –

JENNY. Kids at the high school were seriously pissed about the leak. Like that guy Emily likes? He was real 'political' about it – I'm not sure why he cares so much. I don't know how I feel about the whole 'activism' thing? It's hard to care about someone else's stuff – like the planet? Emily's thinking about being a vegetarian? I think that stuff is kind of a waste of time – you know? Like, we're here, no one has a right to do anything bad to anyone else but why hold up signs and make noise? It's not like you guys *wanted* to spill nuclear stuff –

JOSEPH. It's called trace spillage – these things happen with some frequency actually. We're looking at likely being regulated by the EPA next year as a result of the – accident.

JENNY. Wait – you weren't there were you?

JOSEPH. No.

JENNY. I don't want to get contaminated.

JOSEPH. That's not possible. I'm surprised you know about it. Frankly.

JENNY. Duh. Everyone knows about it.

JOSEPH. It's not a problem.

JENNY. So. What are we going to do?

JOSEPH. This.

JENNY. You aren't going to work?

JOSEPH. *(Deciding.)* No. No. I'm going to take the day off.

JENNY. *(A shocking, exciting realization.)* I'm really not going to school!

JOSEPH. Only this one time.

JENNY. Cool. I'd like to change. I'll need a change of clothes. And some makeup too. Maybe you could – like – buy me some stuff? *(With a smile – flirty.)* ...Hey mister, want to take me to the store?

JOSEPH. Sure.

JENNY. There's a girl at school *(The girl is Jenny.)* who steals makeup for us from Walmart. She steals candy too. She does it for friends but she's cool.

JOSEPH. Stealing is a sin.

JENNY. Uh-huh.

JOSEPH. You shouldn't steal.

JENNY. I said my friend did it not me.

JOSEPH. But if you use something stolen you're just as guilty.

JENNY. How? I didn't take it!

JOSEPH. She steals for *you*.

JENNY. So?

JOSEPH. You *use* her. Which is worse?

JENNY. I don't think she's being *used*.

JOSEPH. What about the Commandments?

JENNY. Wow!! Fine. I get it. No stealing!!

> (**JENNY** *goes into the bathroom and slams the door. She locks the door and pees.* **JOSEPH** *tries the door handle. He walks away. He walks back to the door and tries it again – he rattles it. He walks away.*)

JOSEPH. I don't want to to – hang around – with a girl who smokes and steals.

JENNY. I said it wasn't me!

JOSEPH. *(Sudden decision, walking toward the garage.)* I'm going out – to the store –

> (**JENNY** *opens the bathroom door.*)

JENNY. I want to come.

JOSEPH. No. People will notice – you –

JENNY. Please...

JOSEPH. You shouldn't be out – you should be in school –

JENNY. *(Fake coughing.)* I'm sick.

JOSEPH. Can I trust you?

JENNY. *(Coughing.)* Yes... Yes you can.

JOSEPH. I don't know...

> (*He starts to walk away.*)

JENNY. Please. Please please please Mr...Mr... I want to go to Walmart. Please. I'll be good.

(JENNY crawls across the floor to JOSEPH, hugs his legs, and pulls herself slowly up his body and kisses him.)

JOSEPH. I don't know.

(She kisses him again.)

Still not sure –

(She kisses him again.)

(Exhaling.) Okay. Fine.

JENNY. Really?

JOSEPH. Fine. It's fine. Let's go.

JENNY. Yes!

(JENNY gives him another kiss and a peace sign. They exit the room.)

(Beat.)

(The phone rings in the empty room. It's evening and raining outside exactly as it was in Scene B.)

(They return – both seem happy. JENNY is in new clothes and holding a bag from Walmart. JOSEPH has pizza from Pizza Hut. She dumps out the bag in front of the bathroom mirror [makeup, candy]. She puts on lipstick, mascara, eye shadow, blush...)

That was SO fun! That checkout girl was totally staring at us. She thought you were so fine!

JOSEPH. *(Smiling.)* Eat some pizza before it's cold.

(Tiny pause.)

JENNY. Do you know Samantha Fox?

JOSEPH. No.

JENNY. Really? She's sooo fine – soooo pretty. She wears a ton of makeup. Like this.

JOSEPH. Is she a friend of yours?

JENNY. *(Choking/laughing.)* Lord no. She's a singer. Top 40.

JOSEPH. ??

JENNY. Come on! You know: she sings 'True Devotion'?

JOSEPH. I don't know that song.

JENNY. What about: I surrender to the spirit of the night? *(She imitates an echo:)* Night night night??

> (**JOSEPH** *looks at* **JENNY,** *half a smile on his face. She looks at him and then gets a little self-conscious. A small pause.* **JENNY** *grabs a slice, sits on the couch, and happily eats pizza.)*

JOSEPH. Jenny, I'd like to have sex with you.

JENNY. *(Mouth full of pizza.)* Right now?

JOSEPH. Yes.

JENNY. *(Still eating.)* Okay.

JOSEPH. Have you had many boyfriends?

JENNY. A guy offered me kissing lessons once?

JOSEPH. That's not what I –

JENNY. I've never...

JOSEPH. Are you sure you're ready?

JENNY. Yes. I like you. I really like you.

JOSEPH. I like you too Jenny.

JENNY. Okay. ('Mr. Tom Cruise.')

JOSEPH. I'll be very gentle.

> (*He starts to take his clothes off – folding each item neatly and setting it aside. She doesn't look.)*

JENNY. I don't fit in so much at school. Like, with a clique, you know?

JOSEPH. That's okay.

JENNY. It is?

JOSEPH. I think that means you are your own person. You're very mature for your age.

JENNY. I am. I babysit. This one guy, he has a whole stash of dirty mags and stuff. I've looked.

JOSEPH. Okay. So...this is...this is... So this is okay?

JENNY. Uh-huh...

> (**JOSEPH** *is still.*)

JOSEPH. Say it.

JENNY. This is okay?

> (*She is still eating pizza.* **JOSEPH** *looks at her.*)

If we're going to be doing this I'll need those vitamins you were talking about. And new underwear.

JOSEPH. I'll go back to the store – whatever you want honey.

> (**JOSEPH** *pulls* **JENNY**'s *shirt off over her head as she manages to hold onto the pizza – swapping it from one hand to the other. She wears a worn, bright pink bra.*)

Do you want to lie down?

JENNY. Oh. Okay.

> (**JOSEPH** *turns off the lights.* **JENNY** *lies back. She continues to eat as* **JOSEPH** *pulls her shorts and underwear off.*)
>
> (*She puts the pizza – only crust and one or two bites with cheese left now – onto the coffee table and wipes her hands on the couch. She looks at* **JOSEPH***. He looks at her. She looks at the pizza.* **JOSEPH** *is quiet. They kiss a bit. They have sex.* **JENNY***'s head moves up and down.*)

JOSEPH. I'm just going to put my hand on your neck.

JENNY. Oh. Okay.

> (**JOSEPH** *does – he chokes her a little. She coughs. [Coughs too much for attention and to get him to stop.]* **JOSEPH** *is finished. He gets off her and puts his pants back on. He turns the lights back on.*)
>
> (*He gives her her shirt. She doesn't put it on.*)

JOSEPH. You can finish your pizza now.

JENNY. That's it?

> *(She pulls her underwear and shorts on.)*

JOSEPH. Yeah.

JENNY. *(Laughing.)* That's really it?

JOSEPH. Yes.

JENNY. But that wasn't anything.

JOSEPH. *(Sharply.)* What's that?

JENNY. I just mean. I thought it was going to – I thought – well, it's just Angela Martin said that you see things like colors or – and I didn't see anything.

JOSEPH. That'll happen later.

JENNY. It will?

JOSEPH. *(Dismissive.)* You have to practice – you're a girl – you have to teach yourself, how to see the colors.

JENNY. Want to do it again?

JOSEPH. Now?

JENNY. I guess.

JOSEPH. Not yet. In a minute.

> *(She sits quietly.)*

JENNY. I'm the one with the basement.

JOSEPH. ...??

JENNY. It's *my* basement we watch horror movies in. It's *my* mom that rents them. I do that – kind-of-a-lot? – I tell folks stuff I did like someone else did it, like Emily did it. So...everyone thinks they know Emily but...me... they have no idea.

JOSEPH. *(Getting up.)* So you *are* the thief.

JENNY. Oh. You got me.

> *(**JENNY** smiles and holds her wrists out for handcuffs.)*

JOSEPH. Girls shouldn't do those things. I'm – I have to shower.

JENNY. I'll come –

JOSEPH. I'll just be a minute –

JENNY. Please can I come?

>*(He hands her a can of Pringles.)*

JOSEPH. *(Going to her and kissing her head.)* I'll be right back.

>*(**JOSEPH** goes into the bathroom.)*

>*(Sound of the shower. **JENNY** places the Pringles can between her knees – longways – each end on a knee. She calls **EMILY**. **EMILY** picks up during the first ring. This call is very rapid/overlapping fast, **EMILY** mostly whispering.)*

JENNY. Hey...wow – that was fast –

EMILY. *(Whispering.)* Hey! It's crazy late!! Where ARE you??

JENNY. Are you sleeping with the phone?

EMILY. Adam said he'd call so – *where are you??*

JENNY. He *did*???

EMILY. *Where are you??*

JENNY. I can't tell you but guess what?

EMILY. What?

JENNY. *(With British accent.)* Guess-guess-darling!

EMILY. *(British accent.)* I can't – I can't –

JENNY. I lost it.

EMILY. What?

JENNY. It.

EMILY. Lost what?

JENNY. *It.* I lost it...

EMILY. OH MY GOD!!

JENNY. *(Laughing.)* Angela Martin was so totally wrong.

EMILY. OH MY GOD!

JENNY. It's amazing, as easy as a lie but you do have to practice...

EMILY. Practice what?

JENNY. Doing it.

EMILY. Why?

JENNY. To feel things –

EMILY. WHO did you lose it to?

JENNY. I can't tell you but he is soooo fine you're totally gonna die and be so jealous...

EMILY. Tell me!

JENNY. No. But...do you know what skeet is?

EMILY. What?

JENNY. ...He's kind of like minor-famous...

EMILY. *(Whispering.)* Are you with him now?

JENNY. Yes.

EMILY. Is that why you missed school today?

JENNY. Yup.

EMILY. Where are you?

JENNY. I'm not telling you.

EMILY. Are you okay?

JENNY. Yeah.

EMILY. Are you in trouble?

JENNY. No. Are you?

EMILY. No. Are you going to be at school tomorrow?

JENNY. I'm going to hang up now –

EMILY. Fine. I have to go too!

JENNY. Fine. I'm really hanging up now.

EMILY. Okay.

JENNY. I'm hanging up on you!

EMILY. I *am* expecting a call.

JENNY.	**EMILY.**
Goodbye.	Goodbye.

    (Beat.)

Adam and Emily: Scene C

(Five days later. Monday after school. **EMILY** *is sitting on the couch in the rec room.* **ADAM** *enters with two soda cans.)*

ADAM. Here you be.

EMILY. Thanks.

*(***EMILY*** *takes the Diet Coke. She opens it and licks the top.* **ADAM** *watches her.)*

Did they put my friend Jenny's missing poster up at the high school?

ADAM. Yeah.

EMILY. Yeah. Her mom made those. She's missed four days of school.

ADAM. ...

EMILY. She missed her birthday. Her birthday was Saturday.

ADAM. Maybe she's happy where she is.

EMILY. But why wouldn't she come home for her birthday?

ADAM. After a while, after so many, birthdays are...ugh... hyperbolic...

EMILY. I don't think she ran away. I mean, I hope she isn't angry at me. The police came to my house.

ADAM. What?!?!

EMILY. Yup. I told my mom that Jenny called me and she made me tell Jenny's mom and – and – also what she said? – And so they came and talked to me and my folks – like, me sitting on the couch between my parents – and, like, the policeman kept asking me if she ran away? He kept saying it – like if he said it enough times *I* would say it? You know? If I thought she was mad at her folks? If I thought she was angry? 'Is she a *rebellious* girl? Is she a *wild* girl?'

ADAM. Is she?

EMILY. Does it matter? I think my dad is going to kill me. Jenny loves Diet Coke too.

*(**EMILY** drinks some Diet Coke.)*

And then on Friday, her mom came to our front door looking for me? And she was crying and like really loud and I heard her say 'church friend' but my mom wouldn't even let her mom see me? I don't think she'd run away – or maybe she would for a day or two, but definitely not for *six* days and not – she was *excited* for her birthday.

ADAM. They have that missing poster on tv too. Totally static and silent. It just sits on the screen.

EMILY. My folks don't have a tv.

ADAM. One time I came home early – and my brother and his girlfriend were sitting in here, quiet, staring at the tv. I said 'hey.' They said 'hey.' When I turned to go I realized the tv was off.

*(**ADAM** laughs. **EMILY** laughs.)*

You know what I'm saying?

EMILY. Of course. Makeouts.

*(**ADAM** grins. **EMILY** grins.)*

ADAM. My mom said you were the best dead person she ever saw.

EMILY. What?

ADAM. In the play. My mom saw the play last night and she really liked you.

EMILY. I only had four lines.

ADAM. They were very convincing.

EMILY. Jenny missed it, Jenny missed the play.

ADAM. And you missed the closing party.

EMILY. I think I'm kinda – grounded. I like my paper plate superlative.

ADAM. We always give those. Paper plate awards. Luke usually wins them all.

EMILY. All the girls think he's cute.

ADAM. Yeah? Huh.

EMILY. I heard he got submitted to *Sassy Magazine* to the Sassiest Boy in America contest.

ADAM. He'll win.

EMILY. I can't believe it's almost summer.

ADAM. I can't believe I'm almost done with high school. So-long!

EMILY. I want to dye my hair blonde.

ADAM. Your eyebrows won't match.

EMILY. I gotta do something. I'm gonna burst.

ADAM. Would you like the tv on or off?

EMILY. Off.

ADAM. Okay.

> (**EMILY** *sits on the floor and leans against the couch. She sips her soda.* **ADAM** *stands, looking down at her. He places a hand on her knee and presses her leg to the carpet. He does the same with her other knee. She sits with her legs straight out, sipping her soda; her eyes big and staring at him. She is happy.* **ADAM** *takes the soda and places it on the floor away from them.)*

Let's lie down.

EMILY. Okay.

> (**EMILY** *lies down on her back and* **ADAM** *lies next to her. He runs his hands over her body – over the top of her clothes. He reaches under her shirt. She watches him.)*

> (*He touches her face with his fingertips. She closes her eyes. He puts a finger in her mouth. She sucks on it and opens her eyes. He keeps touching her. He doesn't intend the following to be funny. But it is. Funny.)*

Breathe in – deeply. You are moving something. Nothing is hurt in movement – except animals with serious injuries. Are you an animal with a serious injury?

EMILY. What?

ADAM. Breathe.

> (**EMILY** *tries to breathe but she's stifling the giggles.* **ADAM** *puts his other hand on her to keep her still and continues to touch her.*)

When you breathe you share my air and the movement of everything. Really, breathe! Every time you breathe I breathe (unless one or both of us are holding our breath). Hold your breath.

> (**EMILY** *holds her breath.* **ADAM** *holds his breath. They make faces. They laugh. He continues to touch her.*)

Every time we breathe we are close. No matter where we are in the world.

EMILY. I've never been anywhere in the world.

ADAM. Absorb: revel in the disorder of all this. Say out loud – 'Crazy world. Crazy times.'

EMILY. Crazy world. Crazy times.

ADAM. Scream.

EMILY. Ahh!

ADAM. No, really scream.

> (**EMILY** *screams.*)

That was really good. When you scream you empty your lungs like the sun. And when you finish screaming and you are crying you have to breathe, and when you do, we are close. We. Adam and Emily. And God and everything.

> (**ADAM** *kisses* **EMILY**. *She kisses back. They kiss.*)

My birthday is next Saturday. I'd like to spend the day with you.

EMILY. Really?

ADAM. We're going to drive to Georgia to get a tattoo and later, in the evening, I'm having an IBC Root Beer party. No drinks. Cool?

EMILY. Cool. What time?

ADAM. Well, I'll pick you up around ten in the a.m. Luke's coming too.

> (**ADAM** *stands and offers his hand to* **EMILY.**
> *She takes it and stands as well.*)

EMILY. Could you pick me up down the street from my house?

ADAM. Are we sneaking out missy?

EMILY. Yes. My parents are on lockdown 'cause of Jenny it'll be easier just to lie.

ADAM. On the corner at ten a.m. Glorious list please:

EMILY. Porches –

ADAM. Those blue reflectors in the middle of rural highways that indicate fire hydrants and keep you awake when you are driving long distances, especially at night –

EMILY. Spanish moss –

ADAM. Get out of here, kid. Oh! Wait! The sound of your own blood when you hold a shell up to your ear and the idea that, through this, your blood is the ocean.

EMILY. Is that true?

ADAM. Yes.

> (**ADAM** *kisses* **EMILY,** *and she leaves. He sits on the couch and stares at the not-turned-on tv.*)
> (*Beat.*)

Jenny and Joseph: Scene 3

(Three days earlier. Friday.)

JENNY. Joseph?

JOSEPH. Yeah.

JENNY. What day is it?

JOSEPH. Friday. Friday morning.

JENNY. My birthday is tomorrow.

JOSEPH. Is it?

JENNY. Yup. Fifteen.

JOSEPH. Oh. Wow. Okay.

JENNY. This will be my third day missing school. I feel kind – of bad, like if I was at Emily's I'd still go to school??

JOSEPH. What?

JENNY. I can't stop thinking about my mom.

JOSEPH. You can call her –

> *(He hands her the phone. She calls.)*

JENNY. Hey. Mom. It's me. *(She cries.)* ...I'm sorry... I'm not sure... *(She looks at **JOSEPH**.)* a church friend? *(He shakes his head.)* No... Mom – I said I'm sorry! No no no – I'm gonna be fifteen you can't tell me what to do!!

> *(She hangs up.)*

I hate her.

JOSEPH. You don't.

JENNY. I do. I really do. She called me a slut.

JOSEPH. *(Surprised.)* Why would she do that?

JENNY. I – I – I don't know. I think I should go home now.

JOSEPH. *(Sitting up, alert.)* Jenny –

JENNY. Yeah?

JOSEPH. You know you can't tell anyone about this.

JENNY. What?

JOSEPH. Did you tell anyone about this?

JENNY. What? No.

JOSEPH. Did you call anyone else?

JENNY. No.

JOSEPH. Why would your mom say that?

JENNY. I don't know.

JOSEPH. Think!

JENNY. I don't know.

JOSEPH. *(Standing up.)* Let's go –

JENNY. Now?

JOSEPH. We have to get you home.

JENNY. Okay – yeah – you can meet my mom.

JOSEPH. I just said – you can't tell anyone –

JENNY. Yeah but like – when you take me home, you could explain – so she isn't, like –

JOSEPH. I can't meet your mom, Jenny.

JENNY. Well maybe not today – but –

JOSEPH. No Jenny – not now – not ever – Jenny, listen to me, we can't see each other again.

JENNY. Why not?

JOSEPH. We just can't.

JENNY. Why not?

JOSEPH. Well. We'd probably both get in a lot of trouble.

JENNY. I don't care about that.

JOSEPH. I do.

JENNY. But we're in love.

> *(He touches her face.)*

JOSEPH. Didn't you ever want to have a secret?

JENNY. … (Yes.)

JOSEPH. Right now. This is our secret –

JENNY. I can keep the secret and then we can still see each other. Like on breaks from school –

JOSEPH. No no – it's not like that.

JENNY. Like what?

JOSEPH. Look we got ahead of – I didn't expect to feel – and we've really lost track of time here and this, this situation is not good, not good at all and –

> *(The phone rings. They look at each other. He walks over to the phone and answers.)*

Hello. Hey...sorry I know I – I'm running late and...you did? No I didn't get the mes...no no Doug's got it wrong I was there yesterday – yeah, and the day before – I don't know why he would say –

> **(JENNY** *starts to move toward him – he motions her to be quiet.)*

Oh that's good... *(He smiles and laughs a little.)* ... sounds like fun! ...She did? ...

> **(JENNY** *is trying to wrestle the phone from his hand – pulling it from him – listening to the voice on the other end. He is holding her off.)*

Actually, I was just on my way out – uh-huh late – I will...you too... Bye bye now.

> *(He hangs up.)*

What are you doing?!

JENNY. Who was that?

JOSEPH. Nobody – work –

JENNY. She said 'I love you'??

JOSEPH. You shouldn't have touched the fucking phone –

JENNY. Who was it?

JOSEPH. My wife.

JENNY. Shut up.

JOSEPH. It's true.

JENNY. Where is she?

JOSEPH. Out of town.

JENNY. Where?

JOSEPH. Utah.

JENNY. So you're divorced.

JOSEPH. No. Not – no. She's visiting her family.

JENNY. But what about me?!

JOSEPH. This has been real nice – so nice. But it's impossible. It's – it's not real.

JENNY. Yes it is!

JOSEPH. We've had a great time together. But we have to say goodbye.

JENNY. No!

JOSEPH. You aren't listening.

JENNY. I want to see you again!

JOSEPH. Don't you get it? I'm married.

JENNY. So? You love me. I don't care about your wife.

JOSEPH. (*Pulling her.*) Let's go Jenny –

JENNY. We'll see each other at church!

JOSEPH. Not even at church.

JENNY. I'll find you.

JOSEPH. (*He opens his palms – arms wide – helpless.*) I'll have to pretend I don't know you.

JENNY. I'll grab you – I'll shake you.

> (*She does.*)

JOSEPH. (*Holding her arms.*) Stop Jenny.

> (*She's pounding his chest.*)

JENNY. (*A scream like a child's tantrum – free and total.*) No!!

JOSEPH. Calm down –

JENNY. I get this – for me!

JOSEPH. Calm down Jenny. It has to be this way.

JENNY. (*Pounding him again.*) She said she loves you! You liar!! You – you – hypocrite-two-timer-goddamn –

JOSEPH. Stop it!

JENNY. No!

JOSEPH. (*Losing it a little, yelling as you might do with a child – careful but totally out-of-your-mind angry.*) CALM DOWN NOW!

JENNY. *(Pouting, breaking away from him and sitting.)* No!!

> *(Tiny beat.)*

What if I tell her? I'll tell her!

> *(Tiny beat. He sighs and sits next to her.)*

JOSEPH. If you told my wife it wouldn't help us.

JENNY. But she would leave you – she wouldn't want you –

JOSEPH. I'm not sure what she would do.

JENNY. What?

JOSEPH. *(Tired.)* I really don't know what she would do.

JENNY. But –

JOSEPH. ...We married right out of high school. She's – I don't know. What do we do? You and I?

> *(He looks at her. She looks at him.)*

This is impossible Jenny, this is an impossible situation. I guess I didn't think it through – I fucked up here and I like you Jenny, I do, I love you...but we couldn't keep this up – even if I wasn't married.

> *(Tiny beat.)*

JENNY. *(Super cold.)* Yeah. I guess you did. I mean, I am only fourteen.

JOSEPH. What does that mean?

JENNY. I mean, I guess you could get in trouble for bringing me here, like, without my folks knowing and all –

JOSEPH. What are you doing?

JENNY. I mean we did have *a lot* of sex –

JOSEPH. Jenny?

JENNY. I'm just saying, Mr...maybe you should be sweet to me and maybe you should promise – *for reals* – to see me again or...

JOSEPH. Or what?

JENNY. Or I'll tell – and I don't just mean your wife.

JOSEPH. ???

JENNY. *I'll tell.*

> (**JOSEPH** *looks at her.*)

I'm just sayin', I love you and I want to be with you for just a little longer. Okay?

JOSEPH. What –

JENNY. I'd like you to take me somewhere – together?

JOSEPH. Where? Walmart?

JENNY. No. *Travel* somewhere nice. Somewhere no one knows us and we can go to dinner and pretend to be a real adult couple. Play married.

JOSEPH. What are you talking about?

JENNY. Like a *road* trip? Like we talked about? Like you *promised* me?? Like we can pretend to be famous and together forever...

JOSEPH. Like where?

> (*Tiny pause.*)

JENNY. Jekyll Island, Georgia.

JOSEPH. Why – there?

JENNY. (*Jumping up and down.*) We could go to the water park and they have ghost walks and we could go to Glory Beach. You know about Glory Beach? Where they filmed this movie *Glory*? They man-made that beach for that movie – can you imagine? They even got to *name* it – please please please!!

JOSEPH. Then what?

JENNY. (*Very adult.*) Then I'll go home and I'll tell my folks that's where I was...like, totally all by myself.

JOSEPH. And you want to go now?

JENNY. Tomorrow. For my birthday?

JOSEPH. ...

JENNY. Yes. Yes please.

JOSEPH. All right but then, Jenny, you go home and we never tell anyone.

> (**JENNY** *throws her arms around* **JOSEPH** *and hugs him – he pulls her off to look at her.*)

You have to promise this is our secret.

JENNY. I promise. Okay. *After* Jekyll Island.

JOSEPH. Okay.

> *(She offers him her hand to shake. He does so
> – awkwardly – or she crosses her heart.)*

JENNY. I'll need something to wear.

JOSEPH. I'll get you something –

JENNY. Something nice –

JOSEPH. Okay –

JENNY. Promise?

JOSEPH. Yes.

JENNY. Thank you. Thank you. Thank you.

JOSEPH. It's fine.

> *(**JOSEPH** gets up and walks to the door.)*

JENNY. Where're you going??

JOSEPH. Want a Diet Coke?

JENNY. Okay.

> *(He goes out.)*
>
> *(Beat.)*

Adam and Emily: Scene D

(*Adam's birthday almost a week later. The rec room. Loud music can be heard playing from somewhere downstairs.* **ADAM** *and* **EMILY** *fall over each other through the door.* **EMILY** *is soaking wet, drenched [she went swimming in her clothes] and much more sure of herself.* **ADAM** *appraises her.*)

ADAM. This won't do. You're soaking wet.

(**EMILY** *laughs.* **ADAM** *looks in the boxes lining the wall and finds a shirt. It's black with red stripes and has a big hole in the back.*)

Here ya-are, ma'am. You can borrow my shirt.

EMILY. Thank you very much.

(**EMILY** *puts the shirt on over her head and takes off her wet dress from under the shirt – pushing it through the neck as:*)

I'd never been to the lake at night. I'd never been night swimming. I love those songs you guys played – car doors open, headlights on, all the tape decks blasting the same thing –

ADAM. You didn't have to go in with your clothes on, you know –

EMILY. I know – I saw –

ADAM. So modest –

EMILY. Night swimming – you said – not skinny-dipping –

(**ADAM** *kisses her.* **EMILY** *is dressed in only the shirt and tights.*)

ADAM. I have a tattoo!!

EMILY. I know!! So is the apple a symbol of –?

ADAM. No. Just for its own apple sake.

EMILY. Oh. Luke was worried for you. He's sweet.

ADAM. He's a good friend.

EMILY. I thought he was going to cry – the blood and ink – it was sticking in your belly button.

> (**ADAM** *lifts up his shirt to check his navel.*
> **EMILY** *laughs.*)

ADAM. All good now.

EMILY. And the snake in the corner in that huge tank and the woman with her skinny skinny kids. Did you see her?

ADAM. No.

EMILY. She was outside. Her kids were playing in the dirt. She asked if you were my man. Like real rural: 'That your man?' Why did we drive to Georgia?

ADAM. Tattoos are illegal in this fine state of Cack-a-lack-ee.

EMILY. No!

ADAM. Yes ma'am. And you have to be eighteen in Georgia. I'm eighteen. I can vote. I can get drafted.

EMILY. Too young to drink.

ADAM. I can decide the president or die for this country –

EMILY. But no beer!

ADAM. It's just the beginning. I can go anywhere! I can do anything!

EMILY. I can't wait to go everywhere and do everything. I can't wait to vote.

ADAM. Let's see, that'll be 1993.

EMILY. I'll vote Green Party just to piss off my folks.

ADAM. (*Mock discovery.*) So that's why you have to be eighteen to vote.

EMILY. Ha ha. I'm very mature for my age. Everyone says.

> (*Pause.*)

ADAM. So, what's your birthday present for me?

EMILY. I thought, I've thought about it an awful lot and I want to give you my virginity.

> (*Awkward silence.*)

Take it!

ADAM. I can't do that.

EMILY. Why not?

ADAM. We aren't going to be *this* long enough for me to –

EMILY. To what?

ADAM. I can't. I walk in a week. I'll be going to college soon. And then what?

EMILY. Please.

ADAM. No.

EMILY. I just don't think I will ever feel this way again and I will regret it for the rest of my life if I don't share that with you.

ADAM. Trust me, you'll be okay.

EMILY. I won't.

ADAM. I'm sorry.

EMILY. What if I die?

ADAM. Em –

EMILY. What if there is only this?

I love you, Adam.

Isn't it *my* choice? You always say: make something happen, say what you want…?

ADAM. I can't do that to you. I'm not the guy.

EMILY. Please.

ADAM. No.

EMILY. I thought you might say no, so I got you this.

> (**EMILY** *hands* **ADAM** *a shoe horn tied with a grey ribbon.*)

ADAM. A shoe horn. It's just what I always wanted. Thank you.

EMILY. Welcome.

ADAM. Listen. If we had that kind of relationship, one of two things (or maybe both) would happen – First, I'd ruin you. Second, I'd get restless and dissatisfied – not because of who you are but because of who I am.

EMILY. You won't ruin me.

ADAM. I'm sorry.

EMILY. No. You *couldn't* ruin me. Not possible.

ADAM. Em –

EMILY. I can't be ruined. Not by love. Not in the suburbs.

ADAM. *(Laughing.)* Okay. Okay. Sorry.

EMILY. At least I didn't get you the same present everyone else did.

ADAM. You mean the horn?

EMILY. No!

(*Tiny beat.*)

ADAM. Last year's birthday, Luke and I drove out to the beach with these two girls in our physics class and we all drank a little and then we had sex on the beach. Me and this one girl and Luke and the other girl. It was all of our first times. I wrote a poem about it.

EMILY. You mean 'Proximal-Distal'?

ADAM. *(With surprise.)* Yeah.

EMILY. Did you even know them?

ADAM. Just from class. It was actually one of the girls' idea. It's funny we have Econ together now and we just grin at each other every once in awhile. I like having that secret. Like if you slept with a teacher or something.

EMILY. ...I stole that shoe horn from my dad.

ADAM. You aren't in love with me but I can see that you think that you are. God, I feel like I'm preaching talking to someone so many years younger then me, like maybe I know a whole lot. I'm sorry.

EMILY. Don't be.

ADAM. We should get back to my party.

EMILY. Yeah. Okay.

ADAM. Thanks for the horn.

EMILY. Adam –

ADAM. Yeah?

EMILY. I hope you regret – I hope you regret your choice.

(They return to the party.)

(Beat.)

Jenny and Joseph: Scene 4

(Jenny's birthday, Saturday, almost a week earlier. **JENNY** *and* **JOSEPH** *enter the living room from the garage.* **JENNY** *wears sunglasses with black tape on them, a new dress, and new pantyhose.)*

JOSEPH. Here we are. Jekyll Island.

JENNY. *(Taking off the glasses.)* Were you ever going to take me?

JOSEPH. Yes. I wanted to. But –

JENNY. But what?

JOSEPH. I decided against it.

JENNY. When?

JOSEPH. When what?

JENNY. When did you decide? Right away or just now?

JOSEPH. Oh. Uh. At first I thought maybe we'd go there. I got a map but then I thought, what about the traffic? You know?

JENNY. *Traffic?*

JOSEPH. Yeah. I don't know if you know this but it's 'bout a four-hour drive.

JENNY. That's what I wanted to do. Drive. Out of state. With you.

JOSEPH. I'm sorry Jenny.

JENNY. We were in the car for like, an hour, what did you do, drive around in circles?

JOSEPH. Yeah.

JENNY. For an hour?

JOSEPH. Yeah. I wasn't sure – I'm not sure what to do – We can't be out together –

JENNY. We had a deal.

JOSEPH. I know. But it isn't safe –

JENNY. *(Picking up the phone.)* I'm done with secrets. What's your wife's number?

JOSEPH. I'm not going to do this with you.

JENNY. You said you don't love her?

JOSEPH. I got us pizza and I got you a birthday cake.

> *(He unplugs the phone from the wall.)*

JENNY. Fine! What if I walk outside? What if I walk out your front door and scream like hell?

JOSEPH. You wouldn't do that.

> *(She makes a run for the door. He stands in front of it, barring her way. He holds her wrists.)*

JENNY. *(Screaming.)* YOU SHOULD HAVE TAKEN ME TO GEORGIA!

JOSEPH. This could be a lot different, you know.

JENNY. What's that mean?

JOSEPH. *You* walked out of your parents' front door and got in my car.

JENNY. So?

JOSEPH. What if I wasn't a nice guy?

JENNY. What?

> *(She shakes free of him.)*

JOSEPH. I've been nice to you.

JENNY. …

JOSEPH. Aren't you scared?

JENNY. Of what?

JOSEPH. Of me.

JENNY. No.

JOSEPH. Maybe you should be.

JENNY. Why?

JOSEPH. Does anybody know anybody? Really? I been married ten years. Ten fucking years – excuse me – and I don't know my wife.

JENNY. I'm sorry.

JOSEPH. Yeah. Me too.

JENNY. I'm sorry.

JOSEPH. Yeah. You don't know. Being an adult – sucks. When you're – fifteen?– it's like the future is endless and– like, made just for you and then you grow up and it's every day the same thing, the same small-ass things and everything you thought you knew and understood – it's like it just evaporates –

JENNY. I'm sorry.

(She takes his hand.)

JOSEPH. I got you a cake; I got us pizza; I'm tryin' here... we'll celebrate and then, I'll take you home. Okay?

JENNY. *(She relents.)* Okay.

(He gets down on one knee.)

Joe??

JOSEPH. Happy birthday to you...happy birthday to you... happy birthday to Jen-ny...I love-uh-uh-ove-youooo

*(**JENNY** smiles. He gets the cake out of a bag – a big pink cake – cuts two slices, puts them on paper plates with forks, and hands her one.)*

JENNY. I asked for real jelly shoes and a T-shirt with the beaded fringe bottom like Kristen has. I wonder if my mom got them for me?

JOSEPH. I'm sure she did.

JENNY. You think?

JOSEPH. Yeah.

JENNY. I don't know anymore. I wish I could dance.

JOSEPH. You have other talents –

JENNY. Like what?

JOSEPH. You'll figure it out –

JENNY. Thanks for the cake.

JOSEPH. It's been real nice to be with someone, someone who gets me even just for a couple days.

JENNY. Yeah?

JOSEPH. Yeah. Thank you. Thanks for that.

JENNY. Welcome.

> (*She eats cake.*)

JOSEPH. (*Light bulb!*) You know, that's a talent?

JENNY. What is?

JOSEPH. Making people feel – feel comfortable –

> (**JENNY** *smiles.*)

I'm a nuclear technician. Not an engineer.

JENNY. What?

JOSEPH. Yeah –

JENNY. What's the difference?

JOSEPH. Pay grade. Mostly.

JENNY. Oh.

> (*They eat cake.*)

Did you really go to Hawaii?

JOSEPH. Yeah.

JENNY. Good.

JOSEPH. But –

JENNY. But what?

JOSEPH. (*He kind of laughs.*) For my honeymoon.

JENNY. Oh my god. I hate you!

JOSEPH. You hate me?

JENNY. I hate you! You're fucked!

JOSEPH. This is on you.

JENNY. What?

JOSEPH. Why did you get in the car with me?

JENNY. What?

JOSEPH. You said, 'I think I know what's going to happen with us.'

JENNY. What?

JOSEPH. Come on. Wearing that short skirt – you wanted me from the moment you saw me. You didn't care how old I am or if I was married or what-the-fuck-consequence.

JENNY. That's not true!

JOSEPH. Fucking sucking that Twizzler! You wanted this! Begging me for attention. Begging me for candy and makeup and clothes. I bought you. Might as well spray paint 'slut' on your forehead!

JENNY. FUCK YOU!

(She smashes her cake into his face.)

JOSEPH. *(Really, really angry.)* Why'd you do that? What the –

(**JOSEPH** *starts to chase her around the room. She starts throwing things at him – whatever she can find – cans of Pringles, candy bars – she takes the Bible off the shelf and starts ripping out pages and throwing them at him.)*

JENNY. *(With the Bible.)* You said you loved me God damn it. God damn you. God damn you.

(She's breathless. He catches her and holds her.)

JOSEPH. God can walk on water he doesn't need your damn.

JENNY. *(Laughing.)* Oh my god. Oh my god.

JOSEPH. *(Moving her to the bathroom.)* Let's wash that mouth out –

JENNY. You have cake all over your fucking –

(She is still ripping pages out of the Bible and struggling to get away from him. He is trying to get her into the bathroom. A picture drops to the floor from the Bible. They both freeze. Then she fights like hell and gets away from him long enough to grab the picture and run with it to the other side of the room. He watches her.)

JOSEPH. Give me the picture Jenny.

JENNY. No!

JOSEPH. Give it to me now!

(He starts to chase her – jumping over the couch – they are both really moving.)

JENNY. You have daughters! This is what they look like. Your wife, your daughters. Oh my god – is she ten?? I am going to find them. I am going to find these angel girls and tell them their daddy is a fucking cheater. I'm fifteen you fucker!! I'm going to fuck your life.

(She runs for the door. He lunges at her. She balls the picture up in her fist and he can't get it from her so he picks her up and tries to carry her into the bathroom.)

JENNY.

No – no no – no – let me go – what the fuck are you – you are hurting me you fucking – let me go let me go stop –

JOSEPH.

Shut up just shut up give me the picture – shut the fuck up – give it to me –

(He continues to pull her toward the bathroom. They are in the doorway of the bathroom; she has her legs on either side preventing him from pulling her in, and then she goes limp/loss of breath/quiet.)

JENNY. *(Quietly.)* Oh my god.

JOSEPH. Shhh. Stop it. Stop fighting...stop fighting Jenny... it's okay... I'm going to let you go now. I'm going to let go –

(Beat.)

Adam and Emily: Scene E

*(One year and one month later. ADAM is back
from his first year of college. EMILY is standing
in the rec room. He walks in.)*

EMILY. Hey.

ADAM. Oh! Hey– howdy stranger – come here.

(He hugs her. She is surprised.)

EMILY. I should have called first. I was riding my bike. Your
mom said I could just come up. She's outside. She saw
me.

ADAM. It's okay. It's good to see you. It's been a long time

(ADAM sits.)

EMILY. It has been a long time: one year and one month and
well, today – but who's counting... (Haha...ha.)

ADAM. I was in West Virginia. For the summer – and I
ended up going straight to school so –

EMILY. I know. What were you doing?

ADAM. In West Virginia?

EMILY. Yeah.

ADAM. Shoveling shit and watching the sun rise.

EMILY. What were you actually doing?

ADAM. Working on Matt's uncle's farm.

EMILY. As a summer job?

ADAM. Yeah: scratch for college.

EMILY. Oh.

ADAM. It was so hot Luke was always naked.

EMILY. Oh.

ADAM. We learned how to milk the cow. It's like forever ago.

EMILY. It's not a simile it *was* forever –ago. I didn't hear from
you.

ADAM. Yeah. Sorry about that.

EMILY. I called.

(Tiny beat.)

EMILY. ...And your mom gave me your PO box.

ADAM. Yeah. Thanks for your letters.

EMILY. You got them?

ADAM. Yeah.

(Tiny pause.)

Anything new?

EMILY. I've been finding lots of four-leaf clovers in my front yard. I think we live too close to the river plant. Derek calls me 'clover girl.'

ADAM. What else?

EMILY. I spent last night at a friend's house. I don't smell like me today.

ADAM. Why not?

EMILY. Different soap.

ADAM. Ah-huh.

EMILY. There are no small things, Adam.

ADAM. That's true.

EMILY. I know. I'm quoting you.

ADAM. You are? Oh. Yeah. Huh.

(Pause.)

EMILY. *(Getting up.)* I'll let you go.

ADAM. You don't have to.

EMILY. *(At the door.)* I think, I think I do.

ADAM. Don't go yet. Please.

EMILY. Why not?

(Tiny awkward pause.)

ADAM. I thought when I got to Atlanta I'd call all the famous folks in the phone book and ask them to lunch. You know?

EMILY. I remember. Did you?

ADAM. No.

(Tiny pause.)

EMILY. Jenny's dead.

ADAM. I know.

EMILY. You know they found her body by the creek? Off the road, near the elementary school where we used to swing. Two weeks ago. They were a year too late.

ADAM. I read in the paper that he took her to his house – right here in town? They went to the same church.

EMILY. Her parents knew him.

ADAM. Yeah. And he had a family?

EMILY. Yeah. His wife was the one – called the police.

ADAM. I read that.

EMILY. And he was apologetic? When the police came to his house. That's what they said. He was crying and he just told them where he put her body. And he said, he said, he loved her?

ADAM. Anyway. It's horrible.

EMILY. At her funeral the priest said she was 'stormy.' Sometimes 'sunny' sometimes 'stormy.' What does that mean? Is he saying it's her fault? It's like she's famous now. No one can tell me why.

ADAM. Why what?

EMILY. Why. Why she's dead and I'm not. Why.

ADAM. I don't know what to tell you.

EMILY. Really? You used to have a lot of answers?

ADAM. They said she got in his car and stayed with him – that she chose to be there. I don't get why she would do that.

EMILY. You don't?

ADAM. Do you?

>   *(Tiny pause.)*
>
>   (**EMILY** *looks at* **ADAM** *very pointedly.*)

EMILY. Yeah. Adam. I think maybe I do.

ADAM. Really?

EMILY. Yeah.

ADAM. …

EMILY. I feel guilty. She called me, you know, and I didn't, know– you know? I'm, I don't know – culpable– but– those are your words, aren't they?

ADAM. What?

EMILY. That's what you said. About the swing set. When your swing broke and you fell and also ruined that girl's eye – it wasn't your fault – and you didn't know why you felt guilty about pain you didn't cause? Like why does it hurt that we *aren't* hurt?

ADAM. Oh yeah. God. Sorry. I barely remember that happening. I definitely don't remember telling you about it –

EMILY. Well I remember. I remember everything you said. I can talk like you now. I read the books you told me to and I listened to the music you like. I rode my bike past your house like a hundred times hoping your bus might be there – but it never was. You must love college you never come home.

ADAM. Actually, it's not what I thought...

EMILY. How?

ADAM. I'm failing out.

EMILY. What?

ADAM. Julia takes all my time. I love her. We lie in bed and talk and have sex and she makes me coffee in one of those metal-espresso-single-cup-things – on the stove – and she wears long dresses and I never make it to class.

EMILY. What about school?

ADAM. I'm failing out, Emily.

> (**ADAM** *looks at* **EMILY**.)

Emily.

> (**ADAM** *reaches his hand out to her. She stands, holding his hand.*)
>
> (*Tiny pause.*)
>
> (*The sounds of summer.*)

What are you thinking about?

EMILY. Just. The future. My future...

ADAM. Yeah?

EMILY. Yeah.

> *(He looks at her.)*

ADAM. It's, the future is, not – what – you think it will be – it's...it's nothing–never mind–

> *(**ADAM** is looking at **EMILY** – studying her.)*

You know, you've changed.

EMILY. I'm glad you noticed.

> *(**EMILY** detaches her hand from **ADAM**'s and exits, closing the door firmly behind her.)*

End